SNOW SISTERS

THE EN

Hanna felt the globe tug at her
hands. She started to walk along
the tunnel, taking cautious steps
on the slippery floor. She frowned
as the noise of the waterfall
seemed to get even louder, so loud
it made her want to cover her ears.
"I wonder where it's leading us…"

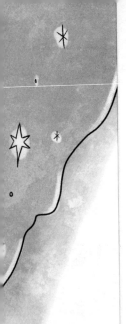

First published in the UK in 2019 by Nosy Crow Ltd
The Crow's Nest, 14 Baden Place
Crosby Row, London SE1 1YW

Nosy Crow and associated logos are trademarks and/or
registered trademarks of Nosy Crow Ltd

Text copyright © Working Partners Ltd, 2019
Cover illustration © Sharon Tancredi, 2019
Interior illustrations © Monique Dong, 2019

The right of Working Partners, Sharon Tancredi and Monique Dong to be
identified as the author and illustrators respectively of this work has been asserted
by them in accordance with the Copyright, Designs and Patents Act 1988.

A CIP catalogue record for this book will be available from the British Library

THE

Printed and bound in the UK by Clays Ltd, Elcograf S.p.A.

Papers used by Nosy Crow are made from wood grown in sustainable forests.

ISBN: 978 1 78800 020 8

www.nosycrow.com

Prologue

The beautiful island of Nordovia, with its snow-capped mountains, glittering waterfalls and sweet-smelling pine forests, was strangely still and silent. The sky was a heavy, dull grey with no hint of the magical Everchanging Lights – the swirling ribbons of purple, pink and blue light that usually danced over the land, bringing peace and happiness. A pale golden sun hovered in the sky but even its rays could not seem to lighten the gloom.

It was the Day of the Midnight Sun, when the sun would reach its highest point and the sky never grew dark. It was usually a day of celebration but now Veronika, the Shadow Witch, had returned. Born into the magical Aurora family, it should have been her duty to protect the Everchanging Lights but instead she planned to steal their magic for herself, plunging the island into darkness and chaos.

Many years ago, Veronika's sister, Freya, had banished her to the remote Svalgard Mountains but now Veronika had come back, stronger than ever and ready to battle for the Lights. She had attacked Freya and her husband, Magnus, but with her last few precious seconds of freedom Freya had magicked the Lights into three beautiful orbs — one purple, one blue and one pink.

Freya had sent the orbs across the land, keeping them safe from Veronika's evil clutches. Beside herself with rage, Veronika had tried to track the orbs down. However, Freya and Magnus's three daughters had beaten her to them. Their quest had been difficult and dangerous but now the Lights were inside a magical snow globe in the girls' castle bedchamber – safe from the Shadow Witch for the moment, at least.

Freya leaned weakly against Magnus. His arm was around her shoulder, his hand stroking her tangled red hair. They were imprisoned in a freezing ice cave carved into the sides of a high mountain in the west. Their faces were creased with worry as they looked out through the one small window across the colourless land. In the far distance they could just make out the silhouette of a castle. Light was shining out of every one of its windows and a circle of blazing orange fires surrounded the walls.

"Our beloved home," whispered Freya.

"The people have lit the lanterns and fires to keep the Shadow Witch away," said Magnus.

"I hope Ida, Hanna and Magda are all safely inside," said Freya.

Magnus rubbed his beard. "Our daughters may be inside at the moment, my love, but we both know they must venture out soon if they are to save Nordovia."

Freya swayed. "I wish I could help them but Veronika has torn most of my magic from me."

Magnus's arm tightened around her shoulders. "You have fought so hard. She has been very cruel to you."

Freya's eyelids fluttered. "I cannot fight for much longer. I am getting weaker all the time."

"Hold on, my love," begged Magnus. "Just for a little longer. Our girls will save the day. I know they will."

A sinister laugh echoed through the icy air and a shape emerged from the shadows at the far side of the cave. "Ah, how sweet," the Shadow Witch hissed. "So, you still believe your daughters can defeat me! Fools."

Magnus's face darkened with fury but as he stepped towards the Shadow Witch she gestured with her hand and an icy blue light shot from her fingers. Magnus stopped dead, frozen in place.

Freya grabbed at his hand. "Magnus!" she

gasped. But he was like a statue – only his eyes moved, frantically. "Veronika! Please, stop this!" Freya pleaded.

"No!" Her sister hissed. "I will do whatever I have to do to get the Lights." She strode to the window and laughed as she looked across the island of Nordovia. "The people believe their lanterns and fires can stop me but nothing will stand in my way. The snow globe can only contain the Lights until the final stroke of midnight tonight. Then when the Lights are released I shall take their power. No one will be able to stop me. I have your magic now as well as my own and I have created an army that obeys my every word."

"Army?" echoed Freya.

"Yes, dear sister! Behold!" The Shadow Witch hissed a spell and a pool of ice appeared at their feet. Its surface showed a swarm of sabre-toothed lions, grizzly bears and silver

wolves. Their eyes glowed red, showing that
they were enchanted by Veronika's evil magic.
Over their heads flew flocks of sharp-beaked
ravens, crows and giant eagles, all with the
same glowing red eyes.

The Shadow Witch's coal-black eyes
glittered. "My terrifying army will storm the
castle, destroying everything and everyone
who gets in their way. They will seize the snow
globe. Midnight will come, and the power of
the Everchanging Lights shall be mine."

Veronika clicked her fingers and the ice
cave was filled with the sound of howls and
snarls and the harsh cawing of vicious birds.
Freya covered her ears at the cacophony.
Veronika cackled and her laughter joined in
with the shrieks and growls, echoing around
the icy walls. Then she clapped her hands
and vanished. The hideous noises stopped and
Magnus was released from the spell that had

been holding him.

He put his arms around Freya. "Did she hurt you, my love?" he asked anxiously.

"No, but Magnus, our poor girls!" Freya's green eyes filled with tears. "How can they succeed in their quest with Veronika's dreadful army against them?"

"Our daughters are brave and their magic grows stronger every day," said Magnus, his eyes looking out of the window towards the castle – a beacon of shining light in the grey landscape. "I believe they will defeat her. We must hold on to our hope."

Freya nodded. "Yes," she whispered. "Hope is all we have left."

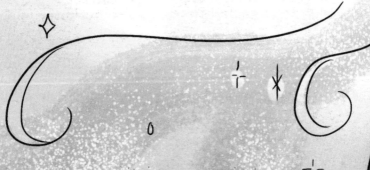

Chapter One

Ida Aurora stood at the window of her
bedchamber in the castle and gazed out at
the gardens below. Lanterns shone from every
tree while servants were hanging silver and
gold bunting around the castle walls and
setting up long trestle tables covered with
gold tablecloths. Madame Olga, the triplets'
governess, kept a close eye on everything.
The cook bustled round, directing the kitchen
boys as they carried huge wicker baskets

filled with fresh bread rolls and mountains of chopped vegetables. Jugglers and stilt walkers were practising their acts and musicians were setting up their instruments.

Every year on the Day of the Midnight Sun there was a grand ball when all the villagers came to the castle for a huge evening feast. At the end of the feast, as the new day began, there was the annual Ceremony of Light where a host of lanterns were released into the sky in a ceremony that celebrated and strengthened the magic of the Everchanging Lights.

Today the preparations were the same as any other year … apart from the fact that there were three times as many guards patrolling the perimeter of the castle walls under the command of Captain Vladimir. Great fires had been lit outside the wall to try to keep the Shadow Witch away.

Ida shivered and glanced down at her long

pink ball dress. "I can't believe the ball is still going ahead this year," she said, turning from the window.

Her sister Hanna was pacing impatiently around the room, the skirts of her shimmering blue ball dress swishing around her legs, while Magda, her other sister, was crouching on the floor in her purple dress, tying a ribbon around the neck of Oskar, their pet Nordovian polar bear cub.

"It's so wrong!" Hanna burst out. "We shouldn't be celebrating while Mother and Father are trapped. We really shouldn't!"

Ida and Magda nodded. The triplets were very different and didn't always agree on things, but they were all in agreement on this.

"I know Madame Olga says it's important to hold the feast and the Ceremony of Light," said Magda. "But I don't want to have to smile and dance and chat to people when Mother and Father are in such danger." Oskar whined anxiously and Magda hugged him. He could grow into a full size polar bear when he wanted to but at the moment he was only the size of a large puppy. "Oh, Oskar, you wish we could find them too, don't you?" she said.

He wuffled in reply and nuzzled her neck
with his dark nose. He missed Magnus and
Freya and wanted them back as badly as the
girls did.

Hanna strode to the centre of the room
where a glass snow globe stood on a wooden
table. Inside the globe, snowflakes swirled
around a crystal-clear waterfall that fell from
a tall cliff into blue sea below. Purple, pink
and blue lights danced through the air inside
the globe.

The snow globe was magical. Their mother
had been able to use it to give the girls clues
about where to find the orbs that contained
the Everchanging Lights. But since they had
found the final orb a few days ago, and had
seen its light being magically absorbed into
the snow globe, they had not heard anything
from her.

"I wish Mother would talk to us again," said

Hanna longingly.

"She's probably too weak," said Ida, feeling her stomach lurch at the thought of their mother in pain, her magic being drained from her by their evil aunt.

Hanna touched the smooth, cold sides of the snow globe. "Tonight, we'll save her and Father," she said, her green eyes flashing with determination.

"We'll take the globe to the Silfur Falls and somehow return the Everchanging Lights to the sky."

"If we can get out of the castle," said Ida, fiddling anxiously with the ends of her long blonde hair. "Madame Olga's been watching us like a snow hawk since we ran away to the Rainbow Springs to find the purple orb last week."

"We'll get out – we have to!" said Magda. "We'll wait until everyone has eaten and the dancing starts and then we'll sneak away."

"Taking the snow globe with us," agreed Hanna. "Then we'll release the lights into the waterfall and they'll return to the sky."

"We don't exactly know how to do that though," said Ida. "Do we go to the top of the waterfall and throw the snow globe into the water? Or do we place it at the bottom of the cliffs where the water falls into Jorin's Pool?"

She frowned.

"Details, details," said Hanna impatiently. "We'll work out what to do when we get there."

"But what if we don't have time when we're there?" protested Ida. "It's going to take ages to travel to the Falls and we've got to put the orb in place by midnight. I'm worried we won't get it right."

"Oh, you're always worried about something," snapped Hanna. "Stop fussing, Ida!"

"Being sensible is not fussing!" declared Ida hotly.

Magda jumped to her feet, wanting to stop her sisters before they argued further. "Maybe Mother will manage to talk to us again before we leave and tell us what to do," she said quickly. "For now, why don't we concentrate on working out how we're going to get out of the castle?"

"Yes. We'll never get out through the main gates," said Ida. "They're too well guarded. You could always change into a bird and fly over the walls," she said to Magda. "But Hanna and I will need to find another way out."

Magda nodded. On their twelfth birthday, each sister had developed magical abilities. It happened to all members of the Aurora family. The sisters each had different powers. Magda could transform into any animal she could see; Ida could draw things which would then become real and Hanna could move things with her mind. Members of the Aurora family all started with one power but could then increase their powers by studying magic and practising their abilities, just like the girls' mother and aunt had done.

"How about we wait until everyone's busy and then we sneak around to the back of the

castle where it's quieter?" suggested Hanna.
"You could draw us a long ladder, Ida, and I
could use my magic to make it stand against
the castle walls so we can climb over. We could
take a rope with us and use it to get down the
other side,"

"Good idea!" said Ida. "Magda could turn
into a bird to keep watch for us and call out
when it's safe and no one is watching."

Magda smiled. "Perfect! We've finally got a
plan!"

"A good one," said Ida, smiling at Hanna,
their argument forgotten.

Oskar whined enquiringly.

Hanna ruffled his ears. "Don't worry. We'll
take you too, Oskar. We'll put you in a basket
and I'll carry you over the wall."

Oskar bounded around in delight. He
grabbed the roll of purple ribbon that Magda
had been using to tie a bow around his neck

and raced off
around the
bedchamber.
It spilled
out, leaving a
trail of ribbon
behind him.

"Oskar, stop!" Magda giggled, trying to
grab him but missing.

Ida and Hanna chased after him. The cub
dodged and swerved, his dark eyes gleaming
cheekily. He ran through Ida's legs, making
her squeal and fall over.

"Got you, you naughty cub!" Hanna
gasped, throwing herself at Oskar and rolling
on the floor with him, just as the door opened
and Madame Olga, the girls' governess,
came in. She was looking as neat and tidy as
ever, her hair in a perfect roll at the back of
her neck, her navy-blue dress spotless. Her

eyebrows rose as she saw Hanna, Magda and
Ida all sprawling on the floor.

"Whatever are you doing?" she exclaimed.
"This is not the behaviour I expect of young
ladies – young ladies who have a grand ball
to attend!"

The girls sheepishly got to their feet.

"Sorry, Madame Olga," said Ida as Magda
quickly started to roll up the ribbon and
Hanna put Oskar in his bed.

"Oskar just got a bit over-excited," said
Hanna, patting the cub.

"Hmm," Madame Olga did not look
impressed. "Well, if he can't behave he'll have
to stay in the stables tonight."

Oskar's ears flattened.

"He'll be fine, Madame Olga. We'll make
sure he's good," said Magda quickly.

"See that you do," said Madame Olga
sharply. "There's quite enough to worry about

without Oskar getting in the way."

"Maybe we should just not have the ball tonight?" Hanna said hopefully.

Madame Olga fixed her with a stern look. "Hanna Aurora, we have been through this before. Cancelling the ball would ruin hundreds of years of tradition and, far worse, send a message to your aunt that we are scared of her. The people of Nordovia will not give in to her evil. Your parents would not want us to."

Hanna bit her lip but didn't say anything more. All the girls knew there was no point arguing with Madame Olga.

"Now, finish getting ready and come downstairs," said Madame Olga. "The guests will be arriving in an hour and you must all be there to greet them with tidy hair and immaculate dresses. You are to behave like perfect hostesses for the night – do you understand?"

"Yes, Madame Olga," the triplets chorused
meekly.

Madame Olga swept out, shutting the door
behind her,

Hanna grinned at her sisters. "We'll behave
like perfect hostesses until we sneak away!"
she whispered.

Magda felt excitement flutter through her
tummy and she squeezed her sisters' hands.
"Then our final adventure to save Nordovia
and Mother and Father will begin!"

Chapter Two

A few hours later, the castle grounds were a picture of festivity. People sat at the tables eating and drinking, the musicians played lively tunes, conjurers entertained the crowds and jesters told jokes. Hanna, Magda and Ida were on their best behaviour, meeting and greeting the guests and making polite conversation with everyone.

"It's almost time to go," Hanna whispered to her sisters as people started leaving the tables and getting up to dance. She pulled a basket out from where she had been keeping it safe under the table. There were three warm coats inside it as well as the snow globe in a special felt bag that Ida had drawn for it. Despite Madame Olga having left them sparkling party shoes to wear, they were all wearing their travelling boots under their long dresses. Luckily Madame Olga had been too busy to notice!

Ida swallowed nervously and glanced around. "Should we see if we can slip away now?"

Magda nodded. "Come on, Oskar," she said in a low voice. "It's time to go." The cub got up and followed her obediently.

The girls put on their coats as they moved through the crowds, heading for the high wall at the back of the castle, but as they got close they heard the sound of shouting from the turrets above. They looked up and saw the guards rushing around, pulling out their bows and nocking arrows ready to fire.

"What's happening?" asked Ida, puzzled.

The enormous warning bell in the watchtower suddenly started to chime. Magda paled. "The castle must be under attack!"

The musicians stopped playing and the guests stopped dancing. In the sudden silence, strange shrieks and screams and howls could be heard on the other side of the castle walls. The ground started shaking as if something very big was approaching. The guards called to each other as Captain Vladimir shouted commands.

"Who's attacking the castle?" said Hanna.

Magda didn't hesitate. "I'll find out!" Seeing a snowy owl flying away from the turrets, she concentrated on its pale form. Magic tingled through her, faintly at first but quickly building up to a rush of power. She felt her body change and shot upwards into the air, powerful white wings beating. For a brief moment, she felt the sheer delight that she always felt when she turned into a bird and was able to fly … but then she remembered why she had transformed. She soared upwards.

Her heart almost stopped beating as she
flew over the turrets. An army of creatures –
wolves, enormous bears, sabre-toothed lions,
all with glowing red eyes – was approaching
the castle across the snowy plains.

Overhead, flying in front of the creatures, were flocks of enormous eagles, crows and ravens, their dark shadows blotting the golden sky. They screamed and cawed as they flew towards the castle, their eyes gleaming viciously, their razor-sharp beaks open and talons outstretched.

Magda felt fear rip through her. With one beat of her powerful wings, she turned and raced back to the ground. She turned back into herself, her wings turning back to arms, her feathers disappearing.

"What is it?" demanded Hanna. "What did you see?"

"Aunt Veronika has sent an army of creatures!" Magda gasped. "She must have put a spell on them because they are so big and their eyes are all red. There are lots of birds too."

"Like the crows we fought at the Rainbow

Pools?" said Ida.

"Like that but there are wolves and sabre-toothed lions too! I couldn't see Aunt Veronika though."

"She's probably controlling them from far away," said Hanna. "The coward! We've got to stop them and—" She broke off as the first flocks of vicious ravens and eagles swept over the castle walls. Hanna quickly pulled the felt bag containing the globe out of the basket and attached it to the belt around her waist. She was going to need her hands free to fight but she wasn't going to leave the globe lying around unattended. It was much too precious. They had to protect it with their lives.

The guests cried out as the birds swooped, attacking with beaks and claws. People tried to fight them off, throwing plates and cutlery and metal goblets. Gregor, the Falconer's apprentice, ran to free the castle hawks from

the hawkery so they could fight back. Torin
the waggoner, and Lars the sleigh driver,
grabbed chairs and used them as weapons,
swiping them at the birds.

The air was filled with the sound of
screaming and shouting. The archers fired
their arrows but there were too many birds
to fight them all off. Guards ran for cover
on the turrets as the birds attacked them
and beneath
everyone's feet
the ground shook
as the rest of the
army approached
the gates.

Oskar roared
and grew to
his full size,
charging at the
birds. The girls

acted instinctively. Magda turned into a
bear just like Oskar and charged at the birds
too, swiping at them with her big paws and
knocking them out so they fell to the ground,
unconscious. She didn't want to kill them
because she knew the birds were not evil
themselves – the Shadow Witch's magic
was making them attack.

Meanwhile, Ida pulled a piece of chalk from her pocket and drew a couple of large nets on the ground. "Hanna! Use these!" she shouted as the magic tingled through her and the nets appeared on the floor.

"Good idea!" Hanna cried. She drew on her own magic and sent the nets flying up into the air. They trapped the birds beneath them, bringing them down to the ground with a thump. The birds' beaks tore at the netting but they couldn't get free.

"To the gates, guards!" Captain Vladimir yelled above the noise. "They're giving way!"

The guards had already barricaded the gates shut but the army of enormous creatures had reached them and were trying to break them down. There was the sound of claws and fangs slashing through wood and the scream of timbers creaking and breaking as the animals pressed against them.

Magda turned back into herself and ran to her sisters. "We've got to do something!" she cried. "This is all our aunt's work. We have to stop her!"

Suddenly the world froze, birds stopping in the air mid-attack, people like statues, mouths open mid-shout. Instead of the noise of the battle there was just an eerie silence. "What's going on?" Ida said, looking round as she realised she and her sisters were the only things moving in the castle grounds.

"Time has stopped," said Hanna. "It must be Aunt Veronika." Anger rushed through her. The ability to freeze time was her mother's main power – their aunt must have taken it from her!

"Oh, my troublesome nieces!" Their aunt's voice tore through the air like an icy wind. "You still think you can stop me – but you have nowhere to run, nowhere to hide. In a few moments, my army will break down the gates and everything you love will be destroyed."

Hanna hugged the snow globe to her chest. "We'll never let you take the Everchanging Lights!"

"You have a choice," their aunt's voice hissed. "Give me the snow globe and I shall call my army off the castle. Refuse to give it to me and everyone here shall die. Do you really want that to happen?" Her voice rose to a shriek. "Decide!"

The girls exchanged looks. What could they do?

Hanna shook her head at her sisters. They couldn't give the Lights to their aunt. They were Auroras. It was their duty to protect them, just as their mother had done. To her relief she saw Ida and Magda shaking their heads too.

"We're not giving up the snow globe!" Hanna raised her voice. "No matter what you do."

"Are you quite sure?" snapped their aunt. "Maybe you need a few more moments to decide." There was a loud crack and time started again. The cacophony of noise hit their eardrums as all around them people and birds started moving again and the gates started creaking and breaking.

Magda grabbed her sisters' arms. "What are we going to do? If we don't give her the globe, everyone here will perish!"

Chapter Three

Hanna looked around at the chaos in the castle grounds. Vicious birds pecked and screeched, people shouted and screamed, and guards raced desperately from the turrets as the castle gates splintered from the creatures' attack. "There must be something we can do to help!" she yelled above the noise. "Can Ida draw a big fire near the gates? Then when the animals come through they'll plunge straight into it."

"But they'd be killed," Magda protested. "It's not their fault they're attacking! They're being controlled."

"I know it's not their fault but we mustn't let Aunt Veronika get the globe," said Hanna.

Magda realised Ida wasn't joining in with their argument. She was crouching down, drawing something on the ground. "What are you doing?" she asked.

Before Ida could reply, a snow globe appeared next to her. It didn't sparkle quite so brightly as the real magic snow globe but in all other ways it looked the same. Ida quickly picked it up.

Hanna frowned. "Why have you drawn a—"

Ida put her fingers to her lips and made a frantic shushing sound. She suspected their aunt could use her magic to listen to what they were saying and if her plan was to work,

then their aunt mustn't know there were two globes.

"Aunt Veronika wants the snow globe," Ida said, looking meaningfully at the new globe and then at the bag tied around Hanna's waist containing the real globe, hoping her sisters would guess her plan. "Well, I think we should give the globe to her." She held out the fake globe.

As she saw Magda's eyes widen and a smile flicker across Hanna's lips, Ida wanted to hug them both. She was sure they had guessed her plan! If they could trick their aunt and give her the fake globe, they might just be able to buy themselves enough time to escape from the castle and get to the waterfall with the real globe. It wasn't much of a plan but surely it was worth a go?

"You're right, Ida," Magda said loudly. "We should give her the globe. It's the only way to save everyone here."

Hanna nodded. "Aunt Veronika!" she
shouted into the air. "You can have the globe
if you stop your army! It's here. Ida's got it –
look!"

There was an ear-shattering screech above
them and then the sound of beating wings
as a dark shadow fell over the girls. They
glanced up, just in time to see a giant golden
eagle flying straight towards them, its claws
open.

Ida expected the eagle to grab the globe
but it didn't. Its talons grabbed the back of
her dress and swept her up into the air, the
globe in her hands. Ida shrieked in alarm. She
hadn't meant this to happen!

"Ida!" screamed Magda and Hanna as the
eagle flapped away with their sister. Oskar,
still in his large form, came charging up and
skidded to a halt beside them. He roared in

dismay as the eagle carried Ida off.

"We've got to go after her!" cried Hanna.

"I know a way. Oskar, you have to shrink and Hanna, you have to grab him!" Before her sister could ask any questions, Magda concentrated on the eagle flying away with Ida and felt her body changing. Her arms became feathered wings, her eyes sharpened, her feet turned to talons. With a screech, she flapped her wings and rose upwards. Hanna picked up Oskar who had quickly shrunk back to a cub. Magda swooped over and grabbed Hanna by the back of her dress just as the other eagle had done then, flapping her powerful wings, she soared up into the sky and headed after the eagle carrying Ida. Hanna gasped, excitement rushing through her as she held Oskar and the bag with the globe in it tightly against her chest.

She looked down at the castle below them. The red-eyed army of creatures was backing away from the gates and the flocks of birds were starting to fly away from the castle, leaving the people to pick themselves off the ground. Hanna realised that now their aunt thought she had the globe heading towards her, she must have lost interest in using up her magic powers to control the army.

We did it, Hanna thought, relief beating through her. *We've saved everyone at the castle.* The icy wind rushed through her short hair and stung her face and arms as Magda, in eagle form, carried her across the snowy plains and over the tops of the pinewoods, but Hanna didn't care about the cold. They had got away from the castle. Now they just needed to get Ida back and then find a way of getting to the waterfall with the real globe.

She knew they were heading into danger but her eyes shone. Whatever was waiting for them, they would deal with it.

The eagle flew on through the skies, heading for the western coast, with Magda following it. She kept her distance, not wanting it to realise it was being followed. Her senses were extra sharp now she was a bird. As she flew over the plains towards the meadows with

their lighter smattering of snow, she could
taste the faint tang of salt on the air and knew
that they were getting close to the sea. Her
pulse quickened. The Silfur Falls fell from the
cliffs into the Western Sea. If they managed to
rescue Ida then there was a chance they could
get to the waterfall by midnight with the real
snow globe!

But she also knew time was passing. The
sun was low in the sky behind them – there
were only a few hours to go until midnight.

Could they do everything
they had to do in the
time left?

We have to! She
thought determinedly.

A snow-capped
mountain loomed up
in front of them and
the other eagle soared
upwards, heading for the
highest peak which stretched up
into the sky.

Magda slowed. She would follow him up
there but she did not want him to realise she
was behind him. Instead she skirted around
the mountain, her wings beating fast. On
the other side of the mountain she could see
clifftops covered with heather and a dusting
of snow. A sparkling waterfall spilled from
one of the cliffs, falling in a bright silver

column into the icy blue sea. The Silfur Falls.
They were so close to them, but first they had
to rescue Ida.

Magda gathered her strength and started to
fly up to the top of the mountain, approaching
from the opposite direction to the other eagle.

She hoped Hanna was OK. Glancing down to her claws, she saw that Hanna's short hair was standing on end from the wind but she looked excited as she gazed around at the landscape beneath her. Oskar seemed to be like a hot water bottle in her arms, keeping her warm.

From the top of the mountain she could see across the whole of the island – from the forbidding mountains and frozen glaciers of the north to the lava fields and hot springs in the east, and across the snowy pinewoods that covered the central region where the castle stood to the warmer western plains beneath them where shaggy ponies grazed, scraping away the thin layer of snow to get to the shoots of sweet grass beneath. Magda's heart sang. Nordovia was so beautiful. She and her sisters had to save it – and their mother and father.

Her sharp ears caught a cry from beneath
her. Glancing down, she saw a platform of ice
at the top of the peak. Around the circle of
ice the snowy sides of the mountain fell away
steeply to a thick ring of thorny bushes. There
was no sign of the other eagle – it appeared to
have flown away. But she did see her aunt –
long, raven-black hair sweeping to her ankles,
an evil smile on her face.

Magda felt a rush of alarm. Ida was lying
at her aunt's feet in a crumpled heap on the
icy ground.

Chapter Four

Ida had the fake globe clutched to her chest. Magda flew silently towards her from above, making sure she stayed behind her aunt. She could hear Veronika laughing mockingly.

"I have you at my mercy," she taunted Ida. "What will your dear sisters be thinking? They'll be out of their minds with worry."

To Magda's relief, Ida moved. She started to sit up. "Let me go!" she said hoarsely.

"No. You will not leave this place. You

should have listened to me when I warned you I would stop at nothing to get the Lights. Now, hand over the globe!"

Ida glared at her and held out the fake globe. Her aunt's eyes gleamed greedily as she hurried to take it. Magda realised this was her chance. She needed to grab Ida while her aunt was distracted. She flew towards them on silent wings. *Ida*, she called in her head. *Ida, we're here!*

Whether Ida sensed she was near or whether she caught the sound of the faint beat of her wings, Magda didn't know, but her sister looked upwards. Seeing Magda and Hanna swooping towards her, Ida's face lit up and as her aunt reached to take the globe, she threw it as hard as she could across the ice. "If you want it, you can go and get it!" she shouted.

The Shadow Witch shrieked in annoyance as the globe bounced away across the icy

ground.
"You fool!"
she snapped,
racing after the
globe. But as she
reached for it, it started to
roll again, moving away from their aunt as if
pushed by an invisible hand. Glancing down,
Magda saw Hanna's eyes were fixed on the
globe. She was moving it using her magic! It
rolled over to the edge of the mountain and

then bounced over the side.

"No!" their aunt gasped as it tumbled down the mountainside before coming to rest deep in one of the thorny bushes.

Magda landed beside Ida and released Hanna just as their aunt swung round. She looked confused as she saw Hanna and Oskar standing next to Ida, with Magda as a giant golden eagle beside them.

"What's happening?" the Shadow Witch demanded. "Why have you brought them here? I didn't tell you to."

Magda realised her aunt thought she was one of her enchanted birds. She took advantage of her confusion and flew at her, her beak open and her talons outstretched.

"What are you doing? Get off me! Go away!" shrieked the Shadow Witch, flapping her hands. She staggered backwards to get away from Magda's claws and tripped over.

The next moment she was tumbling down the snowy side of the mountain. Magda screeched in delight as her aunt rolled over and over in the snow until she came to a jarring stop in the thorny bushes near to the fake globe.

Veronika screamed and thrashed around in fury as the thorns tangled in her cloak and long hair.

"Well done, Magda! Time to get out of here!" Hanna said, running over and hugging Ida.

"I'm so glad you came after me!" Ida gasped. "It was a brilliant idea to turn into an eagle, Magda."

Magda squawked and rose into the air, picking up her sisters, one in each claw. Oskar jumped into Hanna's arms again and Magda flew away from the peak. But strong as she was, it was hard to fly with the weight of Ida, Hanna and Oskar. She doubled her efforts, her wings beating, but she felt her leg muscles straining and her talons aching. *I can't fly all the way to the waterfall*, she realised. *I won't make it.*

She could see the waterfall in the distance, falling from its crest in the clifftop down into the sea, but she could feel herself sinking lower. She tried to flap harder but her wings

were tired now. She was going to have to land.
Spotting a grassy clifftop a safe distance away
from where Aunt Veronika was thrashing in
the brambles, she aimed for it and landed,
her talons giving way and releasing her sisters
and Oskar. As they all tumbled into the soft
heather, Magda felt herself turning back into
a girl. For a moment, she lay there, gasping
for breath. Every muscle in her body ached.
She felt a warm tongue
licking her face
and opened
her eyes to
see Oskar's
concerned
face. She
groaned and
gathered the
furry cub in her
arms.

"Magda, are you all right?" Ida and Hanna crouched down beside her, helping her to sit up.

"Yes, just tired," she gasped.

"You were amazing," said Hanna. "I can't believe you carried me and Oskar all the way here."

"And then rescued me!" said Ida. "I thought Aunt Veronika was going to kill me."

"But I didn't manage to get us all the way to the waterfall," said Magda. She pointed to it in the distance. "The only way to get there is to go across the clifftops but it will take us ages to walk there — we'll never get to it by midnight." For once her usual cheerfulness deserted her and she felt tears fill her eyes.

Hanna hugged her. "We'll think of something."

Ida wrapped her arms around her too. "Don't cry. We can do this."

The sisters hugged each other tightly,
their minds racing. What could they do?
How could they get across the clifftops to the
waterfall?

"WUFF!"

Hearing a loud polar bear bark they
turned and saw that Oskar had grown to his
largest size. He cocked his head on one side
and whined, looking at them and then to the
waterfall and then back to them.

Ida caught her breath. "Oskar wants us to
ride on him! I think he wants to carry us to the
waterfall."

"It will be much quicker if we ride him,"
said Hanna, remembering the times Oskar
had helped them before.

Magda felt new hope fill her, chasing away
her tiredness. She jumped to her feet. "What
are we waiting for? Let's go!"

The sisters ran to the waiting polar bear and

he crouched down as they scrambled onto his soft, warm back – Hanna in the front, then Ida and Magda behind. Hanna held on tight to the thick fur around Oskar's neck.

Oskar stood up and gave an enquiring whine.

"Yes, we're ready!" said Hanna, excitement beating through her. "Come on, Oskar! Go as fast as you can!"

The polar bear leapt forward, his big strides carrying

them across the ground. It wasn't like riding one of the castle ponies. Oskar's back was broad and rolled from side to side with every stride. The sisters hung on tightly as he galloped across the snowy grass.

Maybe we're going to make it. Maybe we're going to get there in time after all! Magda thought in delight.

Chapter Five

Oskar bounded across the clifftops, carrying them closer and closer to the crest of the waterfall. As they got nearer the girls could hear the thunder of the water as it plunged into the sea. The cliffs curved around where it fell, making a semi-circular pool – Jorin's pool, remembered Ida. The deepest pool on the island.

The air around the waterfall was filled with shimmering silvery flecks of light. It was an

awe-inspiring sight.

Oskar stopped a little way from the cascade and the girls climbed off his back.

"It's so beautiful," breathed Magda as she took in the falling water and the silvery light surrounding it.

"It really is." Hanna looked across and saw that the sun was a dark gold orb on the eastern horizon. "But we can't just stand here looking at it. There's hardly any time left until midnight."

They set off across the heather, heading towards the crest of the waterfall. Oskar walked beside them for a few steps but then suddenly tensed and stopped. He swung round, sniffing the air.

"What is it, Oskar?" Magda said.

The hairs on the back of Oskar's neck rose up and he started to growl.

The girls exchanged alarmed looks. Oskar only ever growled when there was real danger. He stalked back the way they had just come, his growling getting louder.

Suddenly Magda's ears caught the faint sounds of howling. Ice seemed to trickle down her spine. There was only one type of animal that made that dreadful noise. "Wolves!" she said anxiously.

"There they are!" cried Hanna as a pack of five wolves burst out of a nearby wood. The wolves streaked across the heather towards them. Their eyes glowed red. Their lips were pulled back to show their sharp teeth.

"Aunt Veronika must have realised we tricked her and sent them to stop us!" said Magda. They were so close to the waterfall. If they ran, maybe they could reach it before the wolves caught up with them. "Quick!"

The three sisters turned and raced across the clifftop towards the silver waterfall. After a few strides, Hanna realised that Oskar wasn't with them. She turned. He was facing the wolves as they charged across the grass towards him. His fur was bristling and there was a fierce look on his usually friendly face.

"Oskar! Come on!" she shouted.

But the polar bear refused to move.

Magda and Ida stopped too. "Oskar, you have to come with us!" Magda begged.

Oskar growled as the first wolf raced towards him. He was a lot bigger than the wolves.

"What are we going to do?" said Ida. "We can't leave him to fight five wolves on his own."

Hanna looked round desperately at the

waterfall. "I know but we have to get the snow
globe into the waterfall. Look how low the sun
is. There can only be about ten minutes left
before midnight."

"Oskar!" Magda cried. "Please! We have to
go!"

But the polar bear was already springing at
the first wolf, knocking it down to the ground
and leaving it winded and gasping for breath.
A second wolf attacked him. Oskar fought

back, snarling and growling. His thick coat seemed to protect him against the wolves' teeth. He swiped out with a heavy front paw, knocking the second wolf out cold.

Hanna grabbed her sisters' hands. "Oskar's giving us a chance. We have to take it and go on to the waterfall. You know we do."

Tears prickling in their eyes, Magda and Ida nodded. They loved Oskar with all their hearts but Hanna was right – they had to try to save Nordovia, and their parents. Swallowing back their tears they turned and ran on to the waterfall.

They finally reached the crest where the water was gushing over the edge of the cliff with incredible force. Standing beside it, the noise of the falling water was so loud it seemed to block out everything else. Spray drenched their hair, their skin, their clothes. Looking over the edge, Ida felt a wave of dizziness as

she gazed at the sea far, far below.

"What do we do with the globe?" shouted Hanna. She took it out of the felt bag and held it up. Its glass sides caught the silvery light and it glittered and glowed. Hanna gasped suddenly. "It feels like it's tugging me!"

"It must be its magic!" said Magda. "Where does it want us to take it?" She glanced behind them, thinking about Oskar. Was he all right? She wanted to get back to him as quickly as possible.

Holding her hands in front of her, Hanna let the globe gently pull her. It guided her across the slippery rocks, closer and closer to the fierce rush of water tumbling over the precipice. Suddenly she felt it shiver in her hands. She stopped and saw a narrow, dark crevice concealed by overhanging rocks. "I think it wants us to go in there," she said.

"Is it the entrance to a cave? Or a tunnel?" asked Ida, peering at it.

Hanna's eyes shone. "I don't know but let's go in!"

"The floor's really slippery," said Magda as she followed Hanna inside. "Be careful."

Ida gasped as her feet slipped on a patch of

thin ice. Magda grabbed her arm and stopped
her from falling over.

"Go slowly, Hanna," Magda begged.

"If you fall the globe might smash," Ida
added.

Hanna was itching with impatience but
she knew her sisters were right and she slowed
down. It was pitch-black inside the crevice
in the rocks and they could hear the thunder
of the waterfall. "I can't see anything,"
Hanna said, raising her voice above the noise,
wondering if she should put the globe back in
the bag so she could use her hands to feel the
way.

But as she spoke the globe started to shine
with a soft, warm light. It glowed like a
lantern, lighting up the gloom.

"We're in a tunnel," Ida said, looking
around at the damp walls. The tunnel seemed
to lead down and round to the right.

Hanna felt the globe tug at her hands again. She started to walk along the tunnel. The others followed, taking cautious steps on the slippery floor.

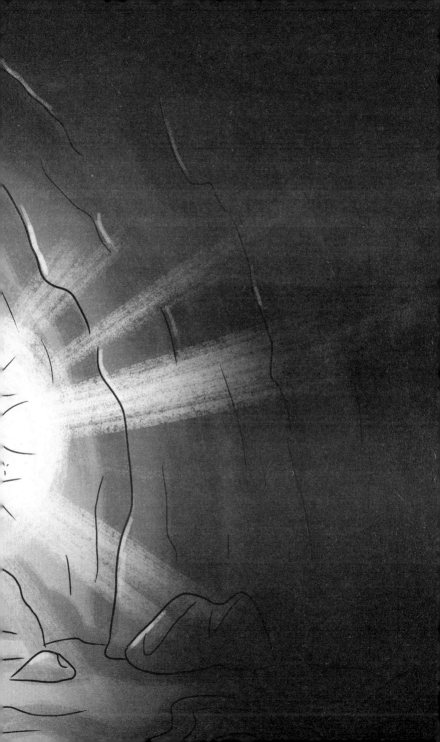

Hanna frowned as the noise of the waterfall seemed to get even louder, so loud it made her want to cover her ears. "I wonder where it's leading us… Oh!" She gasped as she walked around a corner. The rocky wall of the tunnel continued on one side of them but on the other side there was a silver sheet of falling water. They were standing on a platform behind the rocky waterfall, just underneath the clifftop! Silver light danced all around them and far below their feet they could hear the water crashing into Jorin's Pool.

"Oh … wow!" Hanna breathed.

Ida and Magda were both lost for words. They knew without needing to be told that this was a place of deep, ancient magic. They could feel it in the air, and it tingled across the hairs on their skin.

"Look!" breathed Hanna, pointing ahead. There was a circular indent in the rocks at the very edge of the platform. "Do you think we have to put the globe there?"

The globe seemed to shiver in her fingers and once again she felt it tug at her, leading her feet over to the spot she was looking at. "It does need to be put here! It's telling me it does!"

"Be careful, Hanna!" Ida called anxiously. Her sister was very close to the edge and the rocks were very slippery.

Hanna beamed. "I think we've done it! We've got it to the right place with a just a few minutes to spare. We've saved Nordovia!"

A cackle echoed through the air. The shadows on the other side of the platform seemed to move and their aunt stepped out of them. Her hair was tangled with thorns, her cloak ripped and torn. Her black eyes looked wild.

"Not so fast, nieces!" she hissed.

Hanna felt as if a bucket of snow had just been tipped over her. Moving impossibly quickly, her aunt was suddenly beside her, her hands reaching greedily for the globe.

"No!" Hanna shouted, hanging on to it for dear life as her aunt grasped it and tried to tug it out of her grip.

"Let go of it!" the Shadow Witch shrieked.

Hanna was strong but her aunt was even stronger. She wrestled it out of Hanna's grasp just as the sound of the first bells started to ring out across the land to signal that midnight had arrived.

Aunt Veronika's eyes glittered in triumph as she held the globe up. "Now, I have it! The power of the Lights will be mine and everyone will fear me!" she shrieked.

The globe started to shine brighter and brighter. The girls watched in horror as their aunt was surrounded by the glow from the

globe. Power seemed to be pulsing through her.

"No!" shouted Hanna. "We won't let that happen!" She launched herself at her aunt and tried desperately to prise the globe from her grip. They staggered together. Magda and Ida leapt forward to help, but as they collided with Aunt Veronika, her feet slipped. In an instant they all lost their balance and tumbled into the thundering water of the Silfur Falls as the midnight bells continued to ring out across the land.

Chapter Six

Hanna, Magda, Ida and the Shadow Witch were swept downwards in the freezing, thundering waterfall. They were lost in the chaos of water, silver light and thundering noise, unable to even think about using their magic as they tumbled over and over.

Is this the end? thought Magda. *Is this how we die?*

With a painful crash, she hit the surface of the sea and plummeted down into Jorin's Pool, propelled by the force of her fall. Where were her sisters? Where was the globe?

I need air. The thought beat through her, silencing everything else.

Kicking desperately, she fought to halt her downwards plummet. Arms flailing, feet kicking, she swam up towards the surface. Her lungs were burning. Her heart was beating painfully in her chest. She was going to suffocate! Stars started to dance in front of her eyes. Just when she thought she was going to have to open her mouth and breathe in water, she broke through the surface of the pool. Gasping for breath she felt the silvery air fill her lungs. She took two big gasps before the force of the waterfall crashing on her head forced her back down into the depths.

As Magda was pushed downwards she started to panic that she was going to drown but then she realised she didn't have the same feeling of suffocating. The silvery air she had drawn into her lungs at the surface seemed to be helping her to breathe underwater. It must be magic, she realised in amazement. She relaxed in relief and felt herself floating downwards. Her feet touched something hard and she opened her eyes. She expected it to be dark under the water – she knew she was far from the surface – but to her surprise the bottom of the pool was lit by a faint golden glow that seemed to be coming from the sky overhead. She looked down and saw that the base of the pool was a mirror shimmering with magic – a beautiful smooth silvery disc. Relief rushed through her as she realised that Hanna and Ida were at the bottom of the pool too – both were also breathing easily and were looking around, their eyes wide and astonished as the water currents flowed through their hair and moved their long dresses around their legs. Magda spotted her aunt staggering to her feet a little way off and then realised that the light at the bottom of the pool was starting to get brighter and brighter. What was happening?

Glancing up, Magda realised that the extra light was coming from the snow globe. It was tumbling down through the water towards them. The purple, blue and pink lights were swirling around inside it and sparkling as it fell faster and faster. Magda saw her aunt's face crease with rage as she tried to run to catch the globe – but she wasn't fast enough!

The globe smashed down into the rocky floor, exploding in a cloud of pink and purple and blue lights. Veronika collapsed on the floor screaming as the colours danced around the girls. Light seemed to flood into the bottom of the sea from every angle. The girls felt power rushing through them, filling them with light and energy and strength.

The water around them started to swirl and foam and suddenly they were being pushed up towards the surface. They shot out of the water and somersaulted high up into the sky, tumbling through the silvery waterfall and splashing down into the blue ocean safely away from the thundering cascade.

"Look!" gasped Hanna, pointing at the sky as they trod water. The heavy grey colour had disappeared and the sky was now glowing a beautiful bright gold. As they watched, the purple, blue and pink lights swirled upwards out of the water and the whole sky flashed. The girls instinctively shut their eyes because the light was too bright to look at. When they opened

them again, the Everchanging Lights were
dancing in ribbons across the sky.

"We did it!" cried Magda in joy. "The Lights
are back where they should be!"

The three girls swam on the spot as torrents of water continued to pound into the sea beside them. They should have been freezing but the magic that had surrounded them under the water seemed to have banished cold and tiredness. Ida thought she had never felt so warm and alive. She spun round.

"We did it! We did it!" Suddenly she spotted a movement behind the waterfall's spray. "Is that Aunt Veronika?"

They saw their aunt's arm reach out of the water. Her head popped out and she gasped a breath before she was sucked under again. The colour had faded from her face and she looked older and weaker, her hair hanging in thin straggles.

"She's drowning!" said Magda in alarm.

Hanna swam towards the cascade. "We can't just let her die," she said as their aunt surfaced again. "We'll save you!" she shouted. "Ida can you draw some rope?"

Ida nodded. Gathering all her strength, she swam around the side of the waterfall to the rocks behind it. She picked out a sharp stone from inside a crevice and scratched a picture of some rope on the surface of a rock. A coil of rope appeared beside her. She threw it to

Magda who threw it to Hanna.

"Aunt Veronika!" Hanna yelled. "Grab the rope and I'll pull you in." She circled one end of the rope above her head like a lasso and then threw it so that it landed next to their aunt.

"I do not need your help!" their aunt panted, ignoring the rope.

"But you're going to drown!" shouted Hanna.

Aunt Veronika's eyes narrowed. "I said I don't need your help. I still have some power left!" She muttered a spell. At first nothing happened but then she repeated the words and a rope of dark green ivy started to slowly grow at the top of the cliff on the other side of the waterfall. The girls watched as it crept down the cliff. Reaching the bottom, it slithered across the rocks and into the sea. Their aunt splashed wearily towards it and grabbed it.

She used it to haul herself out of the water.
She stood on a rock, panting and bedraggled,
water and seaweed dripping from her hair, her
cloak and dress torn.

"You will be sorry for this, nieces," she cried and, giving them a final bitter look, she stepped into the shadows at the base of the cliff and vanished.

Hanna, Ida and Magda stared at where she had been standing and then Hanna breathed out and swam back to the others. "She's gone."

"For now," said Ida slowly, wondering where her aunt would go and what she would do next.

"She looked different," Magda said. "Much weaker."

"She changed when the Lights went back into the sky," said Hanna. "I don't know why it happened but I hope it means she never threatens Nordovia again."

They all nodded and Magda looked around. "How are we going to get home?" They were treading water at the bottom of the sheer cliff face. It was far too steep and treacherous for them to climb up.

"I'm not sure," said Hanna uncertainly.

Just then Magda saw five large dark shapes moving through the water near the base of the cliffs. What were they? "Narwhals!" she realised as a long straight tusk broke through the water and a pale silvery-grey narwhal surfaced, shooting water from its blowhole.

An idea popped into Magda's head. "Wait! I know how we can get back!" The Narwhal's body sank into the water again but Magda had seen all she needed to see.

She scrambled into the water and thought about the narwhal, about its dappled grey body, its kindly dark eyes, its long spiraled tusk, and she felt herself changing shape.

Hanna gasped. "We're going narwhal riding, Ida!" She grabbed Ida's hand in delight, then the two girls scrambled onto Magda's broad smooth back. Magda plunged away, dipping through the waves, using her strong tail to propel her towards the other narwhals. She clicked her tongue and whistled

in delight as a shoal of silvery fish swooped
past her nose and swirled around her body.
It was so much fun being a sea animal and
the magic that was coursing through her had
swept away all her tiredness!

The other narwhals gave her a surprised
look as she caught up with them but they
seemed happy for Magda and the girls to join

their pod as they swam through the icy ocean, following the coastline. They whistled at Magda and she whistled and clicked back. As they swam around the headland, she spotted a flat stretch of beach leading to low, grassy cliffs.

Hanna and Ida both laughed in delight as Magda clicked goodbye to the pod, put on a burst of speed and raced through the water towards the shore. As she reached it she let the magic go and turned back into a girl. They all splashed in the water together and then, giggling and laughing, they waded out of the water and onto the pale sand.

"That was so much fun!" said Hanna, her spirits restored by the exciting ride.

"Our dresses are totally ruined now though," said Ida as she squeezed the water out of her hair and looked down at her soaking wet, torn dress. "Can you imagine the telling off we're

going to get from Madame Olga when we get back?"

"Who cares?" said Hanna. "We've saved the day!"

Chapter Seven

Talking about everything that had happened, the three sisters set off up the cliff. They were almost at the top when they heard the sound of voices calling their names. They stopped in shock.

"Is... Is that Mother and Father?" Ida stammered, hardly daring to believe it.

There was a barking sound.

"That's definitely Oskar!" cried Magda, her heart leaping.

"We're down here!" shouted Hanna.

The others joined in. "Mother! Father!" they shrieked.

Oskar appeared at the top of the cliff with Freya and Magus beside him. His fur had been torn out in places but otherwise he looked unharmed. Freya and Magnus were pale and disheveled but when they saw the girls their faces lit up with joy. "Girls!" Magnus roared.

Hanna, Magda and Ida squealed in delight and raced to the top of the cliff. Their parents were free! Reaching them, they jumped into their arms.

Their mother's green eyes shone as she stroked her girls' hair and kissed their foreheads. "Oh, my darling girls!"

Their father hugged them all to him while Oskar snuffled at their faces.

"I can't believe you're here!" said Ida.

"It's like a dream come true," said Hanna.

"We've been waiting and waiting to see you again," said Magda. It was all she and her sisters had been longing for since the night their parents had been taken prisoner. "And Oskar, I'm so glad you're all right too." She hugged Oskar tightly. He nuzzled her neck and made a contented wuffling noise.

"We've been so worried about you," said Magnus. "We've been thinking about you every second of every day while we've been trapped."

"How did you escape?" Hanna asked their parents.

"Because of you, my clever girls – you realised what you needed to do and when the snow globe fell into Jorin's Pool and the Everchanging Lights streamed back into the sky, I felt Veronika weaken," Freya said. "So I used the last of my strength to take back the

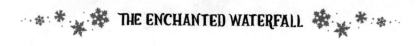

magic she had stolen from me."

"So that's why she looked different?" said Hanna. "Older and frailer?"

"Yes," Freya said. "As her power left her, the ice cave we were trapped in started to melt. We escaped and as we were coming down the mountain we met Oskar and he led us here."

"I think he had smelled us and was coming to see if he could help us," said Magnus, ruffling Oskar's fur. Oskar made a contented grumbling noise and licked their noses. Then he shrank back to cub size. Ida scooped him up and he snuggled into her arms and immediately fell happily asleep.

Magnus and Freya put their arms around their daughters. "We're so very proud of you all," said Magnus. "You've been so brave and clever, and so determined. You have saved Nordovia."

"And us," said Freya, clutching the girls'

hands. The sisters grinned in delight. "It's time to go home," added Freya. "My strength is returning. If we wait a while longer, I'm sure I shall be strong enough to use magic to get us back to the castle in time for the Ceremony of the Lights."

"It's all right, Mother. There's no need to wait. We can help!" said Ida proudly. She knelt down and drew a magnificent sleigh in the snow using a stick. Magic rushed through her, stronger than ever before, and almost before she had finished drawing, the sleigh appeared.

"That's amazing, Ida," Freya cried. "What wonderful magic!"

"And I'll get us some ponies to pull it," volunteered Hanna. She ran across the snowy heather. From her vantage point, she could see a herd of shaggy ponies grazing. She'd never tried to move animals with her mind, but her magic felt so strong now, she was sure it would work.

She concentrated on the ponies and felt the magic spark through her. She focused on two of the ponies and imagined them coming towards her and they did. As if they were pulled by a magnet, they trotted across the heather until they stopped in front of her. They looked confused and snorted in alarm. For a moment, Hanna thought they were going to gallop away but then a third pony appeared from behind Hanna and trotted up to them.

Magda! Hanna realised her sister had transformed into a pony herself. Magda nuzzled the anxious ponies, touching her nose to theirs and reassuring them with gentle whickers and snorts. The ponies relaxed and then followed her over to the carriage. Magda turned back into herself and they stood

quietly, allowing her to attach the harnesses
as she murmured softly to them.

Freya and Magnus shook their heads as
they watched. "Our girls. Our little girls,"
said Magnus in wonder. "You've grown up so
much."

Freya's eyes shone happily. "You're going to
be the most powerful Auroras who ever lived,
I can feel it in my bones." She climbed into
the carriage and smiled. "And now, thanks to
your magic, we can all return home for the
Ceremony of Light!"

Magnus took the reins and the ponies set
off across the plains. The girls snuggled up
to each other and to their mother and Oskar
dozed on Magda's lap. They told their parents
about all their adventures – everything
they had seen and done and learned since
their parents had been captured. As they
approached the castle, the guards on the

battlements spotted them and a cry went up
– first one guard and then another until all
the guards on the battlement were joining in.
Trumpets sounded, the gates were opened and
the villagers and castle servants flooded out to
see Freya and Magnus and the triplets return.

The carriage swept in through the gates.
Everyone surrounded the Auroras, asking
questions, pointing to the sky where the
Everchanging Lights danced and swirled

again, wanting to know what had happened.
The girls leapt out and their mother and
father stood up.

"Nordovia has been saved thanks to our
wonderful daughters!" Magnus shouted above
the din. "The Everchanging Lights are back in
the sky. The Shadow Witch has fled. All shall
be explained. But for now, let the festivities
commence!"

A great cheer went up. The musicians started to play, the servants hurried around, the ponies were taken off to be fed and watered while the villagers set up the tables and chairs again and more food was brought out.

The girls held hands, watching happily as everyone hurried around, beaming with relief and delight.

"Hanna! Magda! Ida Aurora! Where have you been?" Madame Olga's voice echoed across the courtyard.

They swung round guiltily as their governess swept towards them.

"Uh-oh," said Magda, tensing.

"She's going to be really cross with us for disappearing again!" said Hanna.

"I feel awful. She must have been so upset," said Ida.

"Girls, I've been so worried!" Madame Olga cried. "I didn't know what to do when I saw you being carried off by giant eagles!"

"Well, actually one of those eagles was me," Magda admitted.

Madame Olga's eyes bulged. "You, Magda?"

"Yes, Madame. I know it was a little bit dangerous," said Magda. "But I had to be an eagle so we could follow Ida and save her."

"And then she had to be a narwhal," said
Ida.

"And she's been a pony," said Hanna. "Ooh,
and an owl."

Madame Olga looked as if she was about to
faint. "Narwhals? Ponies? Owls?"

"It's a long story," said Magda. "Please
don't be cross with us."

Madame Olga opened her arms and to the
girls' surprise she gathered them into a huge
hug. "I'm not cross, girls. I'm proud," she said,
her eyes filling with tears. "But I'm so pleased
you're home. I don't think my nerves could
have taken much more!"

There was the sound of trumpets playing
a fanfare. "The sun is rising high for the new
day. It's time for the Ceremony of the Lights!"
said Madame Olga, releasing them.

Everyone gathered in the courtyard,
forming a circle. In their hands they all held

paper lanterns. Freya walked to the centre of the circle with an ornate golden lantern in her hands. The colour had returned to her face and she looked strong, proud and happy.

"Girls," she said, beckoning to the triplets who had gone to stand with their father as they usually did at the Ceremony of Light. "You have now come into your powers and so it is time that you join me in the centre of the circle."

Hanna ran into the middle, grinning. Magda saw Ida hanging back, looking a bit embarrassed. Ida hated people staring at her.

"Come on," whispered Magda, squeezing her hand. "If you can fight Aunt Veronika, you can do anything."

Their eyes met, Ida smiled at her and let her sister lead her to the centre of the circle.

A hush fell and Freya spoke.

"My friends, we have faced a great enemy

but she has been defeated. Nordovia is safe again. The Everchanging Lights are back in the sky, bringing happiness and peace to our island. As the new day dawns, we will now perform the Ceremony of Light to strengthen the Lights' magic for the year ahead by sending light and love into the sky." She looked up and waited – one second, two seconds, three seconds…

Suddenly a rose-pink colour flushed across the sky – a beautiful, magical sunrise. There was a collective gasp of breath.

Freya whispered a soft word: "*Frystora!*" and suddenly time froze. Everyone stood perfectly still. The only people still moving were Freya and the triplets.

Freya smiled at her daughters. "I now have my powers back. Your aunt can no longer freeze time. Let us complete the ceremony."

She held the golden lantern out. "Touch the

lantern with me, girls. Shut your eyes and concentrate on those you love. Do not open your eyes until I say."

The girls all touched the lantern and shut their eyes. Pictures swirled through their heads: their mother, their father, Oskar, Madame Olga, each other, the land itself…

On the other side of their shut eyelids they could sense a bright light shining.

"Open your eyes, girls," their mother whispered. They did as she said and saw the lantern was now ablaze with golden light.

Freya blinked and time started moving again. She held the glowing lantern up and all the lanterns around the circle magically lit up too. The people cheered. "Release your light and love into the sky, my friends!" Freya called.

She let go of the golden lantern and it floated upwards. The other lanterns did the same, a multitude of rainbow lanterns, all floating up towards the sky, pulled by magic. Higher and higher they went until they all exploded and disappeared in a single bright flash and the Everchanging Lights doubled in intensity. Magda, Hanna and Ida wanted to laugh and dance and sing. All around them, people were hugging and smiling.

"Light and love in Nordovia for the year ahead," Freya whispered to her daughters. "And the most powerful thing of all – hope."

Magnus came to join them and the Aurora family stood together, arms around each other, watching as the blue, purple and pink Everchanging Lights swirled in their beautiful dance across the Nordovian sky.

The Rescue Princesses

Look out for
another AMAZING
series from Nosy Crow!

Friendship, animals and
secret royal adventures!